I0881182

But I was free, and they should be free.
-Harriet Tubman

I am not afraid I was born to do
-Joan of Arc

I am a queen. And as long as I live, I will reign.
-Zenobia

To create one's world in any of the arts takes courage.
-Georgia O'Keeffe

side of the room and the guys on the other side of the room. I guess they didn't want to associate with me. But I could hold my own with them and sometimes did better. -Mary Golda Ross

A woman is like a tea bag. You can't tell how strong she is until you put her in hot water.
-Eleanor Roosevelt

History's Yearbook

Virginia Loh-Hagan

The world has used me so unkindly. I fear it has made me suspicious of everyone.
-Mary Anning

Liberty!
–Inayat Khan's last word

If you hold your hand closed, nothing good can come in. The open hand is blessed, for it gives in abundance, even as it receives. -Biddy Mason

Girl Spies

I've never been afraid in my life.
-Nancy Wake

I attribute my success to this: I never gave or took any excuse.
–Florence Nightingale

Women should be someone, and not something.
–Mary Cassatt

Well-behaved women seldom make history.
-Laurel Thatcher Ulrich

Here is the day. We must welcome it with song.
–Marie Laveau

The title of Queen rang sweet to my ears.
-Catherine the Great

Contents

Introduction

We are celebrating girl spies! Spies collect and report intelligence. Intelligence means information. Spies take down enemies. Some wear disguises. Some pretend to be other people. Some use special **gadgets**. Gadgets are special tools and machines.

Spies risk their lives. They overcome challenges. Challenges are hard tasks.

But it's not easy being a girl spy. Some people think spying is too dangerous for women. Throughout history, women have shown they're brave. They're strong. They're smart. The girl spies in this book rise to the top. They paved the way for today's girl spies. Spies are more than just secret **agents**, though. Agents are officers. They're loyal. They're creative. They're problem solvers. You just might have the qualities to be the next best spy!

Here's to you and all the girl spies in our lives!

chapter 1

BEST ALL-AROUND

Agent 355

> The Americans did not outfight us, they out-spied us.
>
> –British soldier

The "Best All-Around" award goes to Agent 355! Agent 355 was the best spy. No one knows who she was.

Agent 355 was a code name. Code names are secret names. Agent 355 worked for George Washington. She was part of his Culper Spy **Ring**. Ring means group. Agent 355 worked during the American Revolution. This was the war for independence from England. She discovered a **traitor**'s plans. Traitors are people who betray their countries.

The British caught Agent 355 in 1780. People believe that she was taken on a prison ship. Some say she had a baby boy on the ship. They think she died on the ship.

We don't really know what happened to her. But we do know she's one of the first American female spies.

chapter 2

MOST LIKELY TO COOK UP A PLAN

Julia Child

Learn how to cook. Try new recipes. Learn from your mistakes. Be fearless. And, above all, have fun! –**Julia Child**

The “Most Likely to Cook Up a Plan” award goes to Julia Child. Child was a famous chef. She cooked fancy French food. She had a TV show. She wrote many cookbooks. She was the first woman in the Culinary Institute of America’s Hall of Fame. Culinary means cooking.

She also worked in an intelligence office. Child was a spy. She handled many top-secret papers. She heard top-secret messages. She worked on a sea rescue project. She helped cook up a shark **repellent**. Repellents keep things, like sharks, away.

chapter 3

MOST CLEVER

Barbara Lauwers

> [We were told to] ... work and keep quiet about it. Mind your own business. And don't ask questions. Be available 24 hours a day, 7 days a week.
>
> –Barbara Lauwers

The "Most Clever" award goes to Barbara Lauwers. Lauwers was an American. She was a lawyer. She was a journalist. She spoke several languages. She helped win World War II.

Lauwers was part of an **operation**. Operation means a mission or job. She messed with people's minds. She tricked them. She wrote fake papers. She turned German prisoners into American spies. She had them spread information.

She created the League of Lonely War Women. She tricked German soldiers. She told them lies about their girlfriends. She faked letters. Soldiers got mad. They **defected**. Defect means to quit. These soldiers quit the war. They went back to their homes.

chapter 4

MOST LIKELY TO SIGN UP FOR ANYTHING

Nancy Wake

> I've never been afraid in my life.
>
> **–Nancy Wake**

The "Most Likely to Sign Up for Anything" award goes to Nancy Wake. Wake was born in 1912. She fought against Germans in World War II. She was known as the White Mouse. She escaped traps.

She jumped out of a moving train. Bullets flew past her head. She raided a weapons factory.

She was part of a secret team. She parachuted into France. She jumped out of a plane. She landed using a parachute. Parachutes are cloths that are like big umbrellas.

She rode a bike. She traveled over 300 miles (483 kilometers). She did this in 3 days. She sent a secret message.

chapter 5

MOST LOYAL

Noor Inayat Khan

Liberty!

–Noor Inayat Khan's last word

The "Most Loyal" award goes to Noor Inayat Khan. Khan was Indian and British. She was a princess. She was Muslim. She fought in France. She's the first female radio operator in war. Operators are users. Khan broke codes. She figured out secret messages. She sent reports to England.

Her spy group got caught. Khan didn't run away. She kept working. She was betrayed. She was taken prisoner. She was **tortured** for over 10 months. Torture means to hurt others on purpose. Khan never broke. She didn't tell any secrets.

Some people doubted her. They thought she was too small. They thought she was weak. But she proved them wrong. She was England's first Muslim war heroine.

chapter 6

MOST CHARMING

Zheng Pingru

> I can say that all my family members are patriots.
>
> –Zheng Pingru's sister

The "Most Charming" award goes to Zheng Pingru. Charming means pleasing or delightful behavior. Pingru lived from 1914 to 1940. She came from a rich family. Her father was Chinese. Her mother was Japanese. Pingru lived in China. She could speak both Chinese and Japanese.

Japan invaded China. Pingru sided with China. She became a spy. She spied on the Japanese army. She got intelligence.

She tried to kill a Japanese leader. First, she used her charms. She pretended to like him. She became his girlfriend. Then, she led him to a trap. But the mission failed. She was caught. Her cover was blown. Cover means fake identity. Japanese spies killed Pingru. Pingru risked her life for her country.

chapter 7

BIGGEST TRANSFORMATION

Sarah Emma Edmonds

> I am naturally fond of adventure, a little ambitious, and a good deal romantic. But, patriotism was the true secret of my success.
>
> **–Sarah Emma Edmonds**

The "Biggest Transformation" award goes to Sarah Emma Edmonds. Edmonds dressed in men's clothes. She called herself Frank Thompson. She could do more things as a man.

In 1861, she fought in the U.S. Civil War as "Frank." She was a spy for the Union army. She got information. She stole top-secret papers. She wore many disguises. She colored her skin. She wore a black wig. She pretended to be an African American man named Cuff. She pretended to be an Irish woman. She called herself Bridget O'Shea.

In 1863, she got sick. She left the army. She didn't want to go to the hospital. She didn't want her cover blown.

chapter 8

BEST SURVIVOR

Dahteste

> It is better to have less thunder in the mouth and more lightning in the hand.
>
> –Apache saying

The "Best **Survivor**" award goes to Dahteste. Survivors are people who live through hard times. Dahteste was Native American. She was from the Apache **tribe**. Tribes are groups.

Dahteste spoke Apache and English. Because of this, she became a messenger. She shared messages between the United States and the Apache. She translated. This means she changed words into a different language.

She was a U.S. military **scout**. Scouts are people who find paths, people, or things. She gave the United States information. Dahteste also tried to arrange a peace deal with the United States. She wanted the Apache and the United States to get along. But she was taken to jail. It was unfair. Dahteste spent 27 years in prison. She got sick. She survived. She went back home.

chapter 9

*Mary Bowser, absent on picture day.

BEST TEAM

Mary Bowser and Elizabeth Van Lew

> No pen. No book. No time can do justice to slavery's wrongs, its horrors. –Elizabeth Van Lew

The "Best Team" award was Mary Bowser and Elizabeth Van Lew. Bowser and Van Lew were spies during the U.S. Civil War. They worked for the Union. The Union was also called the Northern Army. They were against the owning of slaves. Bowser and Van Lew lived in the South during the 1860s. Southern people were Confederates. They were for owning slaves.

Bowser was a black woman. She pretended to be a slave. She worked in Jefferson Davis's house. Davis was the leader of the Southern Army. She passed top-secret information to Van Lew's spy group.

Van Lew was a rich white woman. She was from the South. Southern people wanted slaves. But Van Lew was against it. She worked in a hospital for Union prisoners. She passed secret notes. She helped the prisoners escape.

chapter

10

BIGGEST HEROINE

Harriet Tubman

> Every great dream begins with a dreamer.
>
> –Harriet Tubman

The "Biggest Heroine" award goes to Harriet Tubman. Tubman was African American. She was famous for helping slaves. She led slaves to freedom. She knew her way around. She was never caught.

She served as a spy in the early 1860s. She worked for the Northern Army during the U.S. Civil War. She created a spy group. She **recruited** slaves. Recruit means to convince to join. She recruited ex-slaves. Slaves shared information with other slaves. They found out where soldiers left weapons. They found out where soldiers were camped. They found out the movement of soldiers.

Tubman hosted secret meetings. She made secret paths. She kept track of information.

chapter 11

BIGGEST REBEL

Manuela Sáenz

> She really is perhaps the most important woman in Latin American history.
>
> –Venezuelan historian

The "Biggest **Rebel**" award goes to Manuela Sáenz. Rebel means a person who resists. Sáenz lived from 1797 to 1856. She was from Ecuador.

She joined the rebel army. She fought against Spanish rule. She hung out with important people. She was a spy. She held secret meetings. She helped spread information.

She met Simon Bolivar. Bolivar was a leader. He fought for independence from Spain. His enemies tried to kill him. Sáenz saved his life. She became known as the "**Liberator** of the Liberator." Liberator means someone who frees other people.

chapter 12

MOST LIKELY TO WIN AT TRIVIA

Agnes Meyer Driscoll

Fortunate are the people whose roots are deep. –Agnes Meyer Driscoll

The "Most Likely to Win at Trivia" award goes to Agnes Meyer Driscoll. Trivia means interesting facts that are not well-known. Driscoll lived from 1889 to 1971. She was a good student. She graduated from Ohio State University. She studied languages. She studied music. She studied math. She studied science. It wasn't common for women to study math and science at this time. Driscoll liked puzzles. She liked solving things. She became a teacher. She taught math and music.

She joined the U.S. Navy. She was a spy. She worked during both world wars. She broke codes. She invented coding machines. She was known as Madame X. She figured out secret messages from the Japanese Navy. She worked on German codes. She worked on Russian codes.

Advice from the Field

Virginia Hall lived from 1906 to 1982. She was a famous American spy. She went to Turkey. She was in a hunting accident. She lost her left leg. She got a fake leg. She was rejected from being a diplomat because of her leg. But she didn't quit. She got a job with British spies. She did this during World War II. She pretended to be a farmer. She worked in Europe. She organized spy rings. She helped the United States win the war. She was called the most dangerous spy. The Germans put her on their Most Wanted list. She's known as CIA's "Limping Lady." She said, "My neck is my own. If I am willing to get a crick in it, I think that's my prerogative." Crick means a pain. Prerogative means right. Hall advised people to do what they want with their own lives.

Top Memories

- 1779: Peggy Shippen married Benedict Arnold. Arnold was the highest paid spy in the American Revolution. He betrayed the Americans. Some people think Shippen made Arnold do it. They think she sold military secrets to the British.
- 1850: Austria founded the Evidenzbureau. This was the first military intelligence service. It collected information. It sent reports to the leaders.
- 1916: The White Lady was founded. This was a secret spy group. The spies worked in Europe during World War I. They watched the railroads. Over 30 percent of the spies were women.
- May 21, 2018: Gina Haspel became the CIA director. She was the first woman to do so.

Student Life & Clubs

Are you interested in being a spy? Consider going to the International Spy Museum. This museum opened in 2002. It's in Washington, D.C. The museum holds the biggest collection of spy things. It's the only public museum of its type. The museum focuses on how spies shaped world events. People can do fun things at the museum. They can pretend to be spies. They find disguises. They look for hidden cameras. They listen to bugs. Bugs are listening devices. They record secret conversations. People also break codes. They learn to escape. They use spy gadgets. The museum has special programs for youths. There is a Spy-in-Training (SpIT) program. It's for teens ages 15 to 18. The teens help with Spy Camp. They serve as camp counselors. Spy Camp is for youths ages 10 to 13. It hosts spy classes. It hosts real spies as speakers. It hosts spy missions.

"Well-behaved women seldom make history."

–Laurel Thatcher Ulrich

Did You Know...

- Pigeons were used as spies. They sent messages. They took pictures from the air. They guided bombers to their targets.
- The CIA used a cat as a spy. A microphone was placed on a cat's ear. The cat was sent to listen in on Soviets. The cat was hit by a car. The project failed. The CIA has spent over $15 million on it.

Learn More!

Atwood, Kathryn J. *Women Heroes of World War I: 16 Remarkable Resisters, Soldiers, Spies, and Medics*. Chicago: Chicago Review Press, 2014.

Hunter, Ryan Ann. *In Disguise! Undercover with Real Women Spies*. New York: Aladdin; Hillsboro, OR: Beyond Words, 2013.

Lassieur, Allison. *25 Women Who Dared to Go*. North Mankato, MN: Compass Point Books, 2019.

Your Turn!

Now, it's your turn! You get to choose the "Top of the Class: Girl Spy" winner.
Who would you pick?

TOP OF THE CLASS: GIRL SPY

"Top of the Class" means being the best of the best. These prompts will help you think about who'd you pick for the "Top of the Class: Girl Spy" award:

- Why is this person the best "girl spy"? List reasons why this person deserves this award more than others.
- Think about how this person is different from girl spies in this book. What is special about this person?
- How is this person similar to girl spies in this book? Describe the qualities that girl spies should have. How does this person represent those qualities?
- How does this person make the world a better place? How does this person change history? Why should we remember this person?
- Girl spies often struggle. They may also face barriers. They're often told they can't do something. They don't run away when things get hard. How does this person overcome challenges?
- What special skills does this person have? What type of special gadgets does this person have?
- Girl spies blend in. They don't want others to know who they are. How does this person blend in? How well does this person keep secrets?

Consider This!

TAKE A POSITION! Do you think men or women make better spies? What advantages do women have? What advantages do men have? Argue your point with reasons and evidence.

SAY WHAT? Spies live secret lives. They can't tell people who they really are. They have to pretend. Explain how good of a spy you'd be. Describe your spy skills.

THINK ABOUT IT! Experts state there are about 100,000 spies in the United States. They could be from as few as 10 or as many as 80 other countries. What do you think about that? Why are spies important?

Glossary

agents (AY-juhnts) officers or people who work on behalf of another person or group

defected (dih-FEKT-id) quit or left a group or country

gadgets (GAJ-its) tools or machines

liberator (LIB-uh-ray-tur) a person who frees people from others

operation (ah-puh-RAY-shuhn) mission or job

rebel (REB-uhl) someone who resists

recruited (rih-KROOT-id) convinced others to join

repellent (rih-PEL-uhnt) something that keeps things away

ring (RING) group or network

scout (SKOUT) someone who helps find paths, people, or things

survivor (sur-VYE-vur) a person who lives through something hard

tortured (TOR-churd) hurt by someone for a reason or purpose, like to get information

traitor (TRAY-tur) someone who betrays

tribe (TRIBE) a group of people that includes many families who have the same language, customs, and beliefs

Index

45th Parallel Press

Published in the United States of America by Cherry Lake Publishing
Ann Arbor, Michigan
www.cherrylakepublishing.com

Reading Adviser: Marla Conn, MS, Ed., Literacy specialist, Read-Ability, Inc.
Book Designer: Jen Wahi

Photo Credits: ©UtCon Collection/Alamy Stock Photo, cover (left), 10; ©Military History Collection/Alamy Stock Photo, cover (middle), 12; ©Art Collection 4/Alamy Stock Photo, cover (right), 24; ©DonnaHeatfield/Shutterstock, 4; ©Pockygallery/Shutterstock, 4, 8, 18; ©CSU Archive/ Everett Collection/age footstock, 6; ©Everett Historical/Shutterstock, 8; ©History and Art Collection/Alamy Stock Photo, 14; ©Kean Collection/Archive Photos/Getty Images, 16; ©Rothstein, Arthur, photographer/Library of Congress/Reproduction No., LC-DIG-fsa-8b27019, 18; ©Virginia Museum of History & Culture/Alamy Stock Photo, 20; ©Powelson, Benjamin F., photographer/Library of Congress/Reproduction No., LC-DIG-ppmsca-54230, 22; ©Aclosund Historic/Alamy Stock Photo, 26; various art pieces throughout courtesy of Shutterstock

45th Parallel Press is an imprint of Cherry Lake Publishing.

Library of Congress Cataloging-in-Publication Data

Names: Loh-Hagan, Virginia, author.
Title: Girl spies / by Virginia Loh-Hagan.
Description: Ann Arbor, MI : Cherry Lake Publishing, [2019] | Series: History's yearbook | Includes bibliographical references and index. | Audience: Grades 4-6.
Identifiers: LCCN 2019004195| ISBN 9781534147942 (hardcover) | ISBN 9781534149373 (pdf) | ISBN 9781534150805 (pbk.) | ISBN 9781534152236 (hosted ebook)
Subjects: LCSH: Spies--Biography--Juvenile literature. | Women spies--Biography--Juvenile literature. | Espionage--History--Juvenile literature.
Classification: LCC UB270.5 .L64 2019 | DDC 327.12092/52--dc23
LC record available at https://lccn.loc.gov/2019004195

Printed in the United States of America
Corporate Graphics

About the Author:

Dr. Virginia Loh-Hagan is an author, university professor, former classroom teacher, and curriculum designer. She would be a terrible spy. She's loud. She loves to gossip. And she'd spill secrets easily. She lives in San Diego with her very tall husband and very naughty dogs.